Gina D. B. Clemen

Ghastly Ghosts!

鬼魅傳奇

U0108747

商務印書館

This Chinese edition of *Ghastly Ghosts!*
has been published with the written permission of
Black Cat Publishing.

The copyright of this Chinese edition is owned by
The Commercial Press (H.K.) Ltd.

Name of Book: Ghastly Ghosts!
Author: Gina D. B. Clemen
Editor: Alex Smith
Design: Nadia Maestri
Illustrations: Ivan Canu
Picture Credits: Mary Evans/Peter Underwood, Fondazione Magnani Rocca, Fortean
                 Picture Library, Ann Hodgkiss, Kurt Hutton/Hulton Getty, The United
                 States Library of Congress, Cideb archives
Edition: © 2001 Black Cat Publishing
                 an imprint of Cideb Editrice, Genoa, Canterbury

系 列 名：Black Cat 優質英語階梯閱讀 · Level 2
書　　名：鬼魅傳奇
責任編輯：黃家麗
封面設計：張　毅
出　　版：商務印書館 (香港) 有限公司
　　　　　香港筲箕灣耀興道3號東滙廣場8樓
　　　　　http://www.commercialpress.com.hk
發　　行：香港聯合書刊物流有限公司
　　　　　香港新界大埔汀麗路36號中華商務印刷大廈3字樓
印　　刷：中華商務彩色印刷有限公司
　　　　　香港新界大埔汀麗路36號中華商務印刷大廈
版　　次：2014年9月第4次印刷
　　　　　© 商務印書館 (香港) 有限公司
　　　　　ISBN 978 962 07 1703 1
　　　　　Printed in Hong Kong

出版説明

　　本館一向倡導優質閱讀，近年來連續推出了以"Q"為標識的 "Quality English Learning 優質英語學習"系列，其中《讀名著學英語》叢書，更是香港書展入選好書，讀者反響令人鼓舞。推動社會閱讀風氣，推動英語經典閱讀，藉閱讀拓廣世界視野，提高英語水平，已經成為一種潮流。

　　然良好閱讀習慣的養成非一日之功，大多數初、中級程度的讀者，常視直接閱讀厚重的原著為畏途。如何給年輕的讀者提供切實的指引和幫助，如何既提供優質的學習素材，又提供名師的教學方法，是當下社會關注的重要問題。針對這種情況，本館特別延請香港名校名師，根據多年豐富的教學經驗，精選海外適合初、中級英語程度讀者的優質經典讀物，有系統地出版了這套叢書，名為《Black Cat 優質英語階梯閱讀》。

　　《Black Cat 優質英語階梯閱讀》體現了香港名校名師堅持經典學習的教學理念，以及多年行之有效的學習方法。既有經過改寫和縮寫的經典名著，又有富創意的現代作品；既有精心設計的聽、說、讀、寫綜合練習，又有豐富的歷史文化知識；既有彩色插圖、繪圖和照片，又有英美專業演員朗讀作品的 CD。適合口味不同的讀者享受閱讀之樂，欣賞經典之美。

　　《Black Cat 優質英語階梯閱讀》由淺入深，逐階提升，好像參與一個尋寶遊戲，入門並不難，但要真正尋得寶藏，需要投入，更需要堅持。只有置身其中的人，才能體味純正英語的魅力，領略得到真寶的快樂。當英語閱讀成為自己生活的一部分，英語水平的提高自然水到渠成。

商務印書館 (香港) 有限公司
編輯部

使用說明 —————————————

① 應該怎樣選書？

按閱讀興趣選書

《Black Cat 優質英語階梯閱讀》精選世界經典作品，也包括富於創意的現代作品；既有膾炙人口的小說、戲劇，又有非小說類的文化知識讀物，品種豐富，內容多樣，適合口味不同的讀者挑選自己感興趣的書，享受閱讀的樂趣。

按英語程度選書

《Black Cat 優質英語階梯閱讀》現設 Level 1 至 Level 6，由淺入深，涵蓋初、中級英語程度。讀物分級採用了國際上通用的劃分標準，主要以詞彙（vocabulary）和結構（structures）劃分。

Level 1 至 Level 3 出現的詞彙較淺顯，相對深的核心詞彙均配上中文解釋，節省讀者查找詞典的時間，以專心理解正文內容。在註釋的幫助下，讀者若能流暢地閱讀正文內容，就不用擔心這一本書程度過深。

Level 1 至 Level 3 出現的動詞時態形式和句子結構比較簡單。動詞時態形式以現在時（present simple）、現在時進行式（present continuous）、過去時（past simple）為主，句子結構大部分是簡單句（simple sentences）。此外，還包括比較級和最高級（comparative and superlative forms）、可數和不可數名詞（countable and uncountable nouns）以及冠詞（articles）等語法知識點。

Level 4 至 Level 6 出現的動詞時態形式，以現在完成時（present perfect）、現在完成時進行式（present perfect continuous）、過去完成時（past perfect continuous）為主，句子結構大部分是複合句（compound sentences）、條件從句（1st and 2nd conditional sentences）等。此外，還包括情態動詞（modal verbs）、被動形式（passive forms）、動名詞（gerunds）、

短語動詞（phrasal verbs）等語法知識點。

　　根據上述的語法範圍，讀者可按自己實際的英語水平，如詞彙量、語法知識、理解能力、閱讀能力等自主選擇，不再受制於學校年級劃分或學歷高低的約束，完全根據個人需要選擇合適的讀物。

② 怎樣提高閱讀效果？

　　閱讀的方法主要有兩種：一是泛讀，二是精讀。兩者各有功能，適當地結合使用，相輔相成，有事半功倍之效。

　　泛讀，指閱讀大量適合自己程度（可稍淺，但不能過深）、不同內容、風格、體裁的讀物，但求明白內容大意，不用花費太多時間鑽研細節，主要作用是多接觸英語，減輕對它的生疏感，鞏固以前所學過的英語，讓腦子在潛意識中吸收詞彙用法、語法結構等。

　　精讀，指小心認真地閱讀內容精彩、組織有條理、遣詞造句又正確的作品，着重點在於理解"準確"及"深入"，欣賞其精彩獨到之處。精讀時，可充分利用書中精心設計的練習，學習掌握有用的英語詞彙和語法知識。精讀後，可再花十分鐘朗讀其中一小段有趣的文字，邊唸邊細心領會文字的結構和意思。

　　《Black Cat 優質英語階梯閱讀》中的作品均值得精讀，如時間有限，不妨嘗試每兩個星期泛讀一本，輔以每星期挑選書中一章精彩的文字精讀。要學好英語，持之以恆地泛讀和精讀英文是最有效的方法。

③ 本系列的練習與測試有何功能？

　　《Black Cat 優質英語階梯閱讀》特別注重練習的設計，為讀者考慮周到，切合實用需求，學習功能強。每章後均配有訓練聽、說、讀、寫四項技能的練習，分量、難度恰到好處。

聽力練習分兩類，一是重聽故事回答問題，二是聆聽主角對話、書信朗讀、或模擬記者訪問後寫出答案，旨在以生活化的練習形式逐步提高聽力。每本書均配有 CD 提供作品朗讀，朗讀者都是專業演員，英國作品由英國演員錄音，美國作品由美國演員錄音，務求增加聆聽的真實感和感染力。多聆聽英式和美式英語兩種發音，可讓讀者熟悉二者的差異，逐漸培養分辨英美發音的能力，提高聆聽理解的準確度。此外，模仿錄音朗讀故事或模仿主人翁在戲劇中的對白，都是訓練口語能力的好方法。

閱讀理解練習形式多樣化，有縱橫字謎、配對、填空、字句重組等等，注重訓練讀者的理解、推敲和聯想等多種閱讀技能。

寫作練習尤具新意，教讀者使用網式圖示（spidergrams）記錄重點，採用問答、書信、電報、記者採訪等多樣化形式，鼓勵讀者動手寫作。

書後更設有升級測試（Exit Test）及答案，供讀者檢查學習效果。充分利用書中的練習和測試，可全面提升聽、說、讀、寫四項技能。

❹ 本系列還能提供甚麼幫助？

《Black Cat 優質英語階梯閱讀》提倡豐富多元的現代閱讀，巧用書中提供的資訊，有助於提升英語理解力，擴闊視野。

每本書都設有專章介紹相關的歷史文化知識，經典名著更有作者生平、社會背景等資訊。書內富有表現力的彩色插圖、繪圖和照片，使閱讀充滿趣味，部分加上如何解讀古典名畫的指導，增長見識。有的書還提供一些與主題相關的網址，比如關於不同國家的節慶源流的網址，讓讀者多利用網上資源增進知識。

CONTENTS

KET : **K**ey **E**nglish **T**est–style exercises.

This story is recorded in full. 故事錄音
This symbol indicates the beginning of a recording and track number. 錄音和音軌標記

WHAT DO YOU KNOW ABOUT GHOSTS?

1 **Take this test and find out! For each sentence choose either true (T) or false (F).**

	T	F
a. Ghosts are always invisible.	☐	☐
b. Ghosts only live in haunted houses.	☐	☐
c. All ghosts are evil.	☐	☐
d. Ghosts always carry their head in their hands.	☐	☐
e. There are only human ghosts.	☐	☐
f. Ghosts have a strange smell.	☐	☐
g. When you see a ghost your watch stops.	☐	☐
h. Ghosts can move through walls.	☐	☐

2 **Now answer these questions.**

a. Do you believe in ghosts? ☐ Yes ☐ No

b. Are you afraid of ghosts? ☐ Yes ☐ No

c. Does your teacher believe in ghosts? ☐ Yes ☐ No

d. Ask your teacher to describe a ghost.

....
....
....
....

e. Do you believe your teacher? ☐ Yes ☐ No

f. How do you imagine a ghost?

....
....
....
....

GHOSTLY GLOSSARY

Do you know these words? You will find them in the book.

evil = 邪惡的

frightening
= 令人害怕的

demon, 魔鬼

ghastly = 可怕的，
恐怖的

to haunt =（鬼魂）
經常出沒

haunted house,
鬼屋

ghost, 鬼

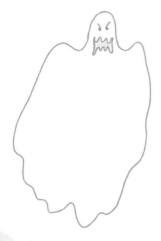

murder = 謀殺

murderer = 兇手

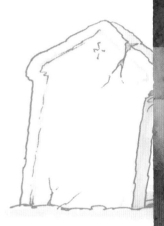

poltergeists = 發出噪音和
亂扔東西的鬼

skull 頭骨

psychic expert = 通靈專家

CHAPTER ONE

What is a Ghost?

enturies ago people talked about ghosts, spirits and spooks, [1] and they still talk about them today. But no one knows exactly what a ghost is!

Certain scientists and psychic experts study ghosts and haunted places. They try to understand supernatural [2] events of the past and present.

Psychic experts use complex machines to discover ghosts. Others try to photograph ghosts. Sometimes ghosts appear in photographs and no one can explain why!

Today several important universities have a Parapsychology [3] Department. In these departments experts study the supernatural and try to find an answer to old questions.

So what is a ghost? The most common explanation is this:

....

1. **spooks**：鬼，幽靈。
2. **supernatural**：超自然的。
3. **Parapsychology**：（此處指）通靈學。

Paranormal Apparitions, Queen's House, 19 June 1966.
Figures photographed on the Tulip Staircase of the Queen's House, Greenwich, England.

Mary Evans/Peter Underwood

GHASTLY GHOSTS!

ghosts are spirits of the dead. Their death was a tragic or terrible one. They haunt the place where they died. It can be a house, a castle, a theatre, a forest, a road or a ship. They cannot rest in peace!

Do ghosts really exist? What do you think? Read this book carefully and become a ghost investigator. [1] Fill in [2] the 'Phantom File' with your opinion after each case... and then decide!

1. **investigator**：調查員。
2. **fill in**：填寫。

UNDERSTANDING THE TEXT

1 **Choose the correct word(s) to complete the sentences.**

a. Psychic experts use complex machines to discover ....

b. Sometimes ghosts appear in ....

c. Ghosts are spirits of ....

d. Psychic experts study ....

1. photographs

2. supernatural events

3. witches

4. ghosts

5. the dead

2 **Odd one out!**

Underline the word that does not belong to the category.

a. spook   ghost   ship   phantom

b. home   castle   house   forest

c. spirit   picture   photograph   painting

d. ghastly   frightening   old   scary

e. university   college   machine   school

f. month   century   year   theatre

3 **Now use the odd words to fill in the gaps.**

a. The scientist used a complex ....

b. The students saw the play at the ....

c. They crossed the sea by ....

d. The castle was very ....

e. Robin Hood and his men lived in the ....

4 **Now make a sentence with the word 'spirit'.**

....

CHAPTER TWO

The Horror of Berkeley Square

There are many ghosts in the city of London. There are haunted houses, theatres, streets and pubs! [1] One of the most evil ghosts is the one at Berkeley Square.

Between 1870 and 1900 no one wanted to live at 50 Berkeley Square. There were footsteps [2] at night and macabre [3] appearances. One particular room in the house was especially dangerous.

In 1870 a brave young man decided to sleep in the haunted room for one night.

'Ghosts don't scare me,' he said.

1. **pubs**：酒吧。
2. **footsteps**：腳步聲。
3. **macabre**：恐怖的，與死亡有關的。

The Horror of Berkeley Square

The next morning he was dead. His body was in the middle of the evil room.

A year later a young girl slept in the haunted room. That night she saw or heard something horrible. The next morning she was

Berkeley Square, London.
Kurt Hutton/Hulton Getty

mad! She could not speak about her horrifying experience to anyone.

Lord Lyttleton was an English lord. 'I don't believe in ghosts,' he told his friends. 'I will sleep in that house and nothing will happen to me.'

During the night the people in the next house heard a gun shot. [1]

The next morning Lord Lyttleton was terrified and told them, 'Something came into the room from that corner. It was slimy [2] and had an evil smell. I fired my gun

Lord Lyttleton

at it and the ghost disappeared. It was horrible! I cannot describe it. That house IS haunted by a ghastly spirit.'

A year later a maid [3] was cleaning the haunted room. She did not know about the evil ghost. At midnight horrible cries came from the haunted room. The people in the house ran upstairs. They found the poor maid on the floor in convulsions. Her terrified eyes stared [4] at a corner of the room. It was the same corner Lord Lyttleton indicated.

1. **gun shot**：槍聲。
2. **slimy**：黏糊糊的。
3. **maid**：女傭。
4. **stared**：瞪眼看。

The Horror of Berkeley Square

The maid refused to speak. Her only words were, 'What I saw was TOO HORRIBLE to describe.' The next morning she died at St. George's Hospital.

The story of the two sailors is perhaps the most famous of all. In 1875 two sailors arrived in London. They wanted to work on a ship. They had no money and nowhere to sleep. They walked around London and came to Berkeley Square.

'Look!' said the younger sailor. 'There's an empty house. We can sleep there.'

The sailors entered the dark, empty house. They went up the stairs.

The older sailor said, 'This house is cold and dark. I don't like it. It scares me.'

'Don't be silly!' said the younger sailor. 'We have nowhere to sleep. Let's stay here!'

They slept in the haunted bedroom. In the middle of the night they both woke up.

'Listen!' said the younger one. 'There's someone downstairs. Can you hear the noise?'

'Yes,' said the other. 'I can hear footsteps. Oh no, the footsteps are coming upstairs!'

At that moment the door opened slowly. A big, dark figure came in. The older sailor was terrified. He could not move. He just sat and looked at the horrible thing.

The younger sailor ran out of the room, down the stairs and out of the house. In the street he found a policeman. They returned to the house, but the sailor was too frightened to enter. The policeman went upstairs alone.

'Is anyone here?' he cried.

There was no answer and he found no one. There was an evil smell on the stairs. He looked everywhere, but he couldn't find the older sailor. Then he looked out of the window. The older sailor was lying in the garden – he was dead.

Did 'something' push him out of the window? Or did he jump out of the window in terror? We will never know.

PHANTOM¹ FILE

NUMBER 1

Where: ....

Name of the haunted place: ....

Number of ghosts: ....

Victims: Yes ☐ No ☐

If 'Yes', how many:.......................................

Your opinion: Haunted ☐ Not haunted ☐

Why: ....

....

....

1. **phantom**：鬼魂。

UNDERSTANDING THE TEXT

KET

1. Are these sentences Right (A) or Wrong (B)? If there is not enough information to answer Right (A) or Wrong (B), choose Doesn't Say (C). Circle the correct answer.

1. No one wanted to live at 50 Berkeley Square because an evil ghost haunted it.
   A Right   **B** Wrong   **C** Doesn't Say

2. All the rooms of the house at Berkeley Square were dangerous.
   A Right   **B** Wrong   **C** Doesn't Say

3. The house was built in the 18th century.
   A Right   **B** Wrong   **C** Doesn't Say

4. Lord Lyttleton believed in ghosts.
   A Right   **B** Wrong   **C** Doesn't Say

5. He fired his gun at the ghost and it disappeared.
   A Right   **B** Wrong   **C** Doesn't Say

6. No one could describe the ghost because it was too horrible.
   A Right   **B** Wrong   **C** Doesn't Say

7. The two sailors came from Scotland.
   A Right   **B** Wrong   **C** Doesn't Say

8. The younger sailor didn't like the house.
   A Right   **B** Wrong   **C** Doesn't Say

9. In the middle of the night the sailors heard footsteps.
   A Right   **B** Wrong   **C** Doesn't Say

10. The policeman found the older sailor dead in his bed.
    A Right   **B** Wrong   **C** Doesn't Say

2 **Listen to the conversation between the two sailors. For each question choose the correct answer A, B or C.**

1. It's a
   - ☐ **A** snowy evening.
   - ☐ **B** windy night.
   - ☐ **C** rainy evening.

2. Both sailors are
   - ☐ **A** thirsty.
   - ☐ **B** hungry.
   - ☐ **C** angry.

3. What time is it?
   - ☐ **A** Half past six.
   - ☐ **B** Six o'clock.
   - ☐ **C** Half past seven.

4. The bakery is near the
   - ☐ **A** square.
   - ☐ **B** school.
   - ☐ **C** church.

5. The older sailor wants to buy
   - ☐ **A** a piece of bread.
   - ☐ **B** an apple.
   - ☐ **C** a big apple pie.

6. The younger sailor wants
   - ☐ **A** a chocolate cake.
   - ☐ **B** a cream cake.
   - ☐ **C** chocolate biscuits.

7. They want to go to the Yellow Duck Tavern because it is always
   - ☐ **A** noisy.
   - ☐ **B** warm.
   - ☐ **C** open.

8. What is the name of the bakery?
   - ☐ **A** Yellow Duck
   - ☐ **B** Church Bakery
   - ☐ **C** Berkeley Bakery

3 **Complete the conversations. For each question choose the correct answer A, B or C.**

1. Can you come to the disco with me?
   - ☐ **A** On Saturday night.
   - ☐ **B** Yes, I went.
   - ☐ **C** Yes, I can.

2. Do you like dancing?
   - ☐ **A** No, I can't.
   - ☐ **B** Yes, I do.
   - ☐ **C** Yes, I have.

3. What time is dinner?
   - ☐ **A** At half past six.
   - ☐ **B** Tonight.
   - ☐ **C** For one hour.

4. Where's your new bike?
   - ☐ **A** Yes, I do.
   - ☐ **B** I have one.
   - ☐ **C** In the garage.

5. How many video games have you got?
   - ☐ **A** Nobody.
   - ☐ **B** Five.
   - ☐ **C** Any.

CHAPTER THREE

Glamis Castle and its Ghosts

Scotland is famous for its haunted castles and its ghosts. Glamis Castle has a long history of violent murders and ghosts. It is a big castle with more than one hundred rooms and many secret hiding places. The castle also hides terrible secrets.

During the Middle Ages there was a battle near the castle. After the battle some men came to the castle. They were afraid and in danger.

'Excuse us, sir. We are in danger. The enemy is following us. Can we stay at your castle for a few days?' they said.

The Earl of Glamis smiled and said, 'Follow me. You can hide in a secret room.'

The men were happy and said, 'Thank you, sir! You are very kind.'

GHASTLY GHOSTS!

The Earl of Glamis looked at the men but did not answer. He took them to a secret room.

'Enter and don't make any noise,' he said.

The men entered. The Earl locked the door and put the key in his pocket. He never opened that door again! Many years later Lord Strathmore opened that door and fainted! [1] He found a room full of skeletons. [2] Visitors to the castle often hear strange noises in that room. They hear knocks at the door. Perhaps the ghosts of the men want to get out!

The 'Grey Lady' is another ghost of Glamis Castle. Lady Janet Glamis lived during the reign of King James V of Scotland. King James was a cruel man and did not like Janet.

'Lady Janet Douglas Glamis is a witch! She tried to poison me!' he said to his court.

'No, that is not true!' cried Lady Janet. 'I am not a witch! I am innocent!'

The King sent poor Lady Janet to prison for many years and she was very unhappy. Then in 1537 the King's men burnt her. Her ghost haunts the clock tower of Glamis Castle. People say her ghost is transparent [3] and there is a strange red light around her head.

At the beginning of the 1800s the Earl of Strathmore had a son. The baby was deformed. [4] The parents hid the baby in a secret room. Only the parents and the nurse knew about the baby.

---

1. **fainted** : 暈倒。
2. **skeletons** : 骸骨。
3. **transparent** : 透明的。
4. **deformed** : 畸形。

GHASTLY GHOSTS!

The boy grew up but he always stayed in the secret room. No one knew the terrible secret. One day a workman went to repair the roof. [1] From the roof he saw the window of the secret room and looked inside.

He was terrified and began to shout, 'There's a strange creature [2] in that room! What people say is true!'

The Earl heard him and said, 'Listen carefully. You saw nothing!'

'But, sir, I did... I saw a.............!'

'You saw no one and heard nothing. Do you understand? I am sending you and your family away from Scotland.'

Glamis Castle

1. **roof** : 屋頂。
2. **creature** : 生物。

Glamis Castle and its Ghosts

'I don't want to go away, sir.'

'Take your family and go to Australia. Here is lots of money. Now go!'

The next day the workman and his family left Scotland.

The creature died when he was very old. Perhaps his skeleton is still in the secret room.

Today people at the castle can hear a child crying at night. Others say that the ghost of a strange creature walks around the castle and makes unusual noises.

PHANTOM FILE

NUMBER 2

Where: ....

Name of the haunted place: ....

Number of ghosts: ....

Victims: Yes ☐ No ☐

If 'Yes', how many:..................................

Your opinion: Haunted ☐ Not haunted ☐

Why: ....

....

....

UNDERSTANDING THE TEXT

1 **Answer the questions by inserting the correct letter in the correct box.**

1. Where is Glamis Castle? ☐

2. Where did the Earl of Glamis put the key to the secret room? ☐

3. What did Lord Strathmore find in the secret room many years later? ☐

4. How did Lady Janet Glamis die? ☐

5. Who haunts the clock tower of Glamis Castle? ☐

6. What did the workman repair? ☐

7. Where did the Earl send the workman and his family? ☐

A

Australia

B

C

D

Scotland

E

F

G

2 **Look at these sentences from Chapter Three.**

The King sent poor Lady Janet to prison for many years and she was very unhappy.
(unhappy = not happy)

Others say that the ghost of a strange creature walks around the castle and makes unusual noises.
(unusual = not usual)

The prefix UN before a word means NOT.
Look at this example:

After the party the house was untidy. =
After the party the house was not tidy.

Use the prefix UN to create new words from the ones given in the sentences.

a. The land in America was not explored.

....

b. The Earl of Glamis was not kind.

....

c. The trip to Spain was not necessary.

....

d. They were not able to help the workman.

....

e. The animals at the zoo were not healthy.

....

f. The secret of Glamis Castle is not known.

....

g. The door of the house was not locked.

....

3 **Now choose a word with the prefix UN and make your own sentence.**

....

....

CHAPTER FOUR

Borley: a Haunted Village

Borley is a small village about 100 kilometres northeast of London. It has a church, a rectory [1] and a few houses. It also has more ghosts than any other village in England!

In 1863 Reverend Henry D. Bull built the Borley Rectory. When he died in 1892 his son became minister and lived in the rectory with his wife and daughters. On 28 July 1900 Reverend Bull heard a noise outside the rectory. He opened the door and saw his daughters. They were very frightened.

'We saw a ghost!' they cried. 'It was a nun [2] – a young nun. She was silent and very sad. She walked in front of us.'

'Where is the ghost now?' asked Reverend Bull.

---

1. **rectory** : 神父或牧師的住宅。
2. **nun** : 修女。

GHASTLY GHOSTS!

'She disappeared,' said one of the girls.

Some people did not believe the girls. But a doctor and a teacher saw the same nun on the same day, 28 July, a few years later. On 28 July 1972 a group of scientists saw her too!

The nun was not the only ghost of Borley Rectory. There was also a headless [1] man, a phantom coach [2] with two horses and others. Other bizarre happenings at Borley included organ music playing in the empty church, lights that went on and off, furniture that moved and stones that fell from the sky!

Reverend Guy Smith arrived at Borley Rectory in 1928. He and his wife didn't like the noises and the other strange events.

'I don't believe in ghosts. It's all a lot of nonsense. But I want to understand what is happening,' said Reverend Smith.

So he called Harry Price to investigate. Price was a famous psychic expert. He arrived at Borley with several assistants and started investigating.

On 10 June 1929 there was a sensational [3] newspaper article in the *Daily Mirror* about

---

1. **headless** : 無頭的。

2. **coach** : 四輪馬車。

3. **sensational** : 引起轟動的。

Borley:
a Haunted Village

Borley Rectory, Essex.
The ghost of the nun was seen near the gate.

Fortean Picture Library

the ghostly figures at Borley. Hundreds of curious visitors came to Borley Rectory. They wanted to see the ghosts! Reverend Smith did not like all these visitors. He soon left. But Harry Price continued investigating. He wrote books about the rectory and its ghosts.

Soon Reverend Foyster and his family arrived at Borley.

He and his family had the same problems as the other reverends. [1] He kept a diary of the bizarre [2] events. During this time mysterious messages appeared on the walls of the rectory. They were written to the reverend's wife Marianne.

Who wrote these messages? Was it a ghost? Or was it Mrs Foyster?

After five years and about 2000 ghostly appearances, Reverend Foyster left Borley! He was the last reverend at Borley Rectory. No one wanted to live there.

On 27 February 1939 a big fire destroyed the rectory. After the fire workmen found a woman's skull in the ground and several religious symbols. People said the ghosts moved to the church after the fire.

But WHY is Borley haunted? Why does the nun appear to many people in the village? Who are the other ghosts?

A legend says the rectory was built on the ruins [3] of a medieval monastery. Near the monastery there was a convent. A monk fell in love with a young nun at the convent. On the night of 28 July they decided to escape together in a coach. But the nuns of the

---

1. **reverends** : 教士。
2. **bizarre** : 古怪的。
3. **ruins** : 廢墟。

Borley Rectory, Essex.
Fortean Picture Library

GHASTLY GHOSTS!

convent discovered their plan. They were very angry. They shut the young nun in a small room and she starved to death. [1] The monk was beheaded. [2]

During the 1960s a psychic expert called Geoffrey Croom-Hollingsworth was interested in Borley. He and his assistant Roy Potter spent a lot of time there.

This is what Croom-Hollingsworth said, 'One summer night I saw the nun walking across the garden. I called Roy Potter and he saw her too. She was about 4 metres from us. Then she disappeared into a wall.'

Croom-Hollingsworth and Potter studied the bizarre events at Borley for many years. Their conclusion? Borley is haunted!

PHANTOM FILE

NUMBER 3

Where: ....

Name of the haunted place: ....

Number of ghosts: ....

Victims: Yes ☐ No ☐

If 'Yes', how many:.................................

Your opinion: Haunted ☐ Not haunted ☐

Why: ....

....

1. **starved to death**：餓死。
2. **beheaded**：被斬首。

UNDERSTANDING THE TEXT

1 **Read the paragraph and choose the best word (A, B or C) for each space. The first is done for you.**

Borley is a village ¹......^B........ 100 kilometres northeast of London.

²................ 28 July 1900 Reverend Bull's ³................ saw the ghost of a ⁴................ . Other people ⁵................ the ghost a few years later. There ⁶................ other ghosts too. The *Daily Mirror* wrote ⁷................ the ghosts at Borley.

Reverend Smith called Harry Price to ⁸................ . ⁹................ messages appeared on the walls of the ¹⁰................ and other strange things happened. ¹¹................ wanted to live there.

1. A few	**B** about	**C** by
2. A On	**B** At	**C** In
3. A wife	**B** sons	**C** daughters
4. A horse	**B** nun	**C** monk
5. A sees	**B** seen	**C** saw
6. A was	**B** were	**C** is
7. A from	**B** by	**C** about
8. A investigate	**B** investigation	**C** investigated
9. A Funny	**B** Long	**C** Mysterious
10. A rectory	**B** church	**C** monastery
11. A Someone	**B** No one	**C** Anyone

2 **What does Geoffrey Croom-Hollingsworth say to Roy Potter? Complete the conversation by inserting the correct letter in the correct box.**

Geoffrey: Roy, where are you?

Roy: 1. ☐ ....

Geoffrey: Can you come upstairs?

Roy: 2. ☐ ....

Geoffrey: Have you got your glasses on?

Roy: 3. ☐ ....

Geoffrey: Can you see the ghost of the nun?

Roy: 4. ☐ ....

Geoffrey: Are you scared?

Roy: 5. ☐ ....

Geoffrey: Let's write this down in our diary. What's the date today?

Roy: 6. ☐ ....

A Yes, I've got them on.

B I'm not afraid of ghosts.

C No, I'm not.

D Today is 28 July.

E I'm downstairs in the study.

F Yes, she's walking on the grass near the gate.

G Yes, I'm coming.

Word Square

**Find the names of three psychic experts and circle them in red.
Then find the names of three Borley reverends and circle them
in black.**

A	D	G	E	P	V	L	K	J	F	Y	R	C
H	O	L	L	I	N	G	S	W	O	R	T	H
C	S	B	Z	N	D	H	O	Q	Y	H	J	A
X	L	D	E	G	L	C	W	K	S	T	G	I
O	Y	F	L	P	C	Z	E	N	T	I	S	Z
H	E	M	J	Q	O	S	S	I	E	N	M	X
Z	O	G	A	E	F	T	G	Z	R	A	I	H
K	I	N	C	R	O	G	T	C	I	S	T	O
R	V	I	O	U	D	R	U	E	V	Q	H	A
M	R	Z	T	B	U	L	L	U	R	V	O	R
P	X	M	F	S	R	U	B	A	L	O	B	W

 Use some of the words you circled to answer these questions.

a. Who was the last reverend at Borley?
....

b. Who saw the nun walking across the garden?
.... and
....

c. Who built the rectory in 1863?
....

d. Who wrote books about the rectory and its ghosts?
....

e. Who called a psychic expert?
....

CHAPTER FIVE

Royal Ghosts

oday the Tower of London is a popular tourist attraction. Millions of people visit it every year. Do they know the Tower is haunted by royal ghosts? William the Conqueror wanted a castle and a prison, and built the Tower of London in 1078. The Tower has a ghastly history of tortures, murders and executions.

Anne Boleyn is a very active royal ghost. In 1533 she became King Henry VIII's second wife. But Henry soon got tired of her because she did not give him a son.

In 1536 Henry decided to marry another woman. He accused Anne Boleyn of treason [1] and put her in the Tower of London. She was beheaded on Tower Green in May 1536. (see map page 45)

Her ghost is white and transparent. She haunts Tower Green, the White Tower and the church in the Tower. Sometimes she

---

1. **treason** : 叛國。

Royal Ghosts

appears with her head. At other times she holds her head in her hand!

The ghosts of Henry's other unlucky wives – Catherine Howard and Jane Seymour – haunt Hampton Court Palace, just outside London.

In 1972 a nine-year-old girl visited the Tower of London with her father.

The tourist guide said, 'Anne Boleyn and other royal prisoners were beheaded on Tower Green. The executioner [1] used a big axe [2] to cut off their heads.'

'That's not true! I saw Anne Boleyn a minute ago. But the executioner did not use an axe because Anne Boleyn was a queen. He used a special sword from France.'

The other visitors were surprised. The little girl was right.

'How do you know this?' asked her father.

'I saw the whole execution on Tower Green a few minutes ago!' she said.

Perhaps the most famous ghosts of the Tower are the two princes. They were heirs to the

Place of execution

Tower Green

White Tower

Bloody Tower

Lieutenant's House

River Thames

---

1. **executioner**：劊子手。
2. **axe**：斧頭。

Royal Ghosts

English throne. When Edward V became King of England in 1483, he was only twelve years old and his brother Richard was ten. Their uncle Richard wanted to be King of England. He took the princes to the Tower and soon they disappeared.

People began asking questions, 'Where is young King Edward, where is his brother?'

People said that Richard was responsible for the murder of the princes.

Then one night a soldier saw two children at the bottom of the stairs. They had long white nightclothes. They looked at the soldier silently. They were very sad and frightened. Suddenly they

Tower of London

disappeared. Then the soldier understood. The children were the ghosts of the two princes. Many people saw the two ghosts at the bottom of the stairs and people still see them now.

In 1647 workmen found the skeletons of two children under the stairs. The skeletons were buried immediately. On windy nights the ghosts of the sad princes still haunt the Tower of London.

The Tower is a very spooky place at night!

PHANTOM FILE

NUMBER 4

Where: ....

Name of the haunted place: ....

Number of ghosts: ....

Victims: Yes ☐   No ☐

If 'Yes', how many: ....

Your opinion: Haunted ☐   Not haunted ☐

Why: ....

....

....

UNDERSTANDING THE TEXT

1 After her visit to the Tower of London, the nine-year-old girl writes a letter to her best friend. Complete the letter by writing one word for each space.

Dear Michelle,
Yesterday I visited the [1]...................... of London with my
[2]...................... and something very strange happened to me.
The tourist [3]...................... said that an executioner used a big
[4]...................... to cut off Anne Boleyn's [5]...................... . But
that isn't true because he used a special [6]...................... from
France. I know this because I saw Anne Boleyn's [7]......................
on Tower Green! The other [8]...................... were surprised.
            See you soon,
            your friend, Jennifer

2 The two princes are in the Tower of London. Listen to what they say and then complete the form.

TOWER OF LONDON

Room:[1] ....

Window(s):[2] ....

Furniture:[3] ....

Number of meal(s):[4] ....

Food:[5] ....

Number of guard(s):[6] ....

49

SOME and ANY

Look at these sentences from exercise 2.

We have some bread and some milk.
We haven't got any toys to play with.

We generally use SOME in affirmative sentences and ANY in negative or interrogative sentences.

He has some free tickets to the rock concert.
Have you got any new CDs?
I can't find any books in the box.

Fill in the gaps with SOME or ANY.

a. Their house hasn't got .... furniture.

b. The boys were hungry and ate .... fruit.

c. Are there .... children in the school?

d. .... tourists visited the castle.

e. Has she got .... money?

f. We can't see .... shops in the village.

g. There is still .... cake on the kitchen table.

Now write a sentence with SOME and one with ANY.

....

....

....

....

....

CHAPTER SIX

American Spooks

Ghosts, spooks, poltergeists [1] and phantoms are part of America's past and present. Halloween is the festivity of ghosts and the supernatural, and as you know, it is celebrated on October 31.

The Winchester Mystery House in San Jose, California, is the spookiest American monument to ghosts. It is a famous tourist attraction and people say that mysterious spooks live there.

Sara Winchester was part of the rich Winchester family. The family made Winchester rifles in the 1800s. During the nineteenth century these rifles killed many people.

When Sara Winchester's husband and baby daughter died, she was very unhappy. Strange things were happening to her. She went to a psychic expert and asked for help.

The expert told her, 'The spirits of the people killed by a Winchester rifle are angry with you. They want revenge!' [2]

1. **poltergeists**：發出噪音和亂扔東西的鬼。　2. **revenge**：報復，報仇。

GHASTLY GHOSTS!

'What can I do?' Mrs Winchester asked.

The expert answered, 'The spirits want you to build a big home for them. You must follow all their instructions. And you cannot rest – you must work seven days a week.'

A view of Winchester Mystery House, San Jose.

Mrs Winchester bought a house in the country. For thirty-eight years she built a home for ghosts! She and the workmen worked seven days a week. She lived in the haunted house and every evening she wore a long blue dress and had dinner and secret meetings with the ghosts. They gave her instructions for building the strange house. Every night she slept in a different bedroom.

Today the Winchester Mystery House has 160 rooms and is

similar to a maze. [1] There are stairs that go nowhere, doors that open onto walls and a window in the floor! Thirteen was a favourite number of the ghosts because there are thirteen bathrooms and all the stairs have thirteen steps.

Nathaniel Hawthorne

Nathaniel Hawthorne was born in Salem, Massachusetts in 1804. He was a famous American writer. His grandfather was a judge [2] at the Salem witch hangings. [3] He was very interested in ghosts, evil spirits and demons.

Every evening after work Hawthorne went to the Atheneum Library to read the newspaper. Reverend Harris went to the Atheneum Library too. He was an old minister of the church. Hawthorne saw Reverend Harris every evening for many years. But they were not friends.

One evening a friend of Hawthorne said, 'Reverend Harris died last week.'

'What? Are you sure?' Hawthorne asked.

'Yes, of course,' his friend answered and went away.

'How is that possible? I saw Reverend Harris at the library this evening and all last week,' Hawthorne thought.

1. **maze** : 迷宮。

2. **judge** : 法官。

3. **hangings** : 絞刑。

American Spooks

For many weeks Hawthorne saw Reverend Harris at the library. He sat in his usual chair and read the newspaper. But the other people at the library could not see him! Hawthorne said nothing to the others.

He was afraid to talk to the ghost. He was also afraid to touch it. After about a month the ghost started looking at him.

'Why is Reverend Harris' ghost looking at me? Perhaps he wants to say something,' Hawthorne thought.

He was confused. He saw the ghost and did not know what to do. One evening he went to the library and Reverend Harris' chair was empty. Hawthorne never saw the ghost again.

Abraham Lincoln

For years he thought, 'Why did I see Reverend Harris' ghost? Why didn't the other people see him?'

Hawthorne thought about Reverend Harris' ghost for a long time, but he was never able to solve the mystery.

The White House in Washington D.C. is also a haunted house! The ghosts of assassinated [1] American Presidents haunt it. Abraham Lincoln's ghost is the most famous. Lincoln was President of the United States during the American Civil War. Many Americans loved him, but he had dangerous enemies too. He stopped slavery in America, but the southern states did not agree with this.

1. **assassinated** : 被暗殺的。

GHASTLY GHOSTS!

The White House in Washington D.C.

On 5 April 1865 Abraham Lincoln had a very bad dream. He was at the White House and he heard people crying in the next room. He got up and went to the East Room. He saw a coffin[1] in the middle of the room. Many people walked by the coffin.

'Who is inside the coffin?' he asked a man.

'The President of the United States, sir. An assassin killed him!'

'What?' said Lincoln. He looked inside the coffin and saw his own body. He was DEAD! He suddenly woke up. He was very scared about this dream. He told his wife and friends.

....

1. **coffin** : 棺材。

American Spooks

On 15 April 1865 Lincoln and his wife went to the theatre. He wanted to relax after a long day. At the end of the performance John Wilkes Booth shot the President in the back of the head! The President of the United States was dead!

Was Lincoln's dream a coincidence? Or did he have supernatural powers?

In the 1920s President Coolidge's wife saw Lincoln's face at the window of the Oval Office. He was very sad.

In the 1930s Queen Wilhelmina of the Netherlands was a guest at the White House. One evening she heard a knock at the door. She opened it and saw Lincoln's ghost. He looked at her and then walked away.

In the 1980s President Reagan's daughter saw Lincoln's ghost too. Today people at the White House still see his ghost in the East Room, in the Oval Office and in the halls.

PHANTOM FILE

NUMBER 5

Where: ....

Name of the haunted place: ....

Number of ghosts: ....

Victims: Yes ☐   No ☐

If 'Yes', how many:....................................

Your opinion: Haunted ☐   Not haunted ☐

Why: ....

....

....

UNDERSTANDING THE TEXT

1 Mike and Sue are at the Winchester Mystery House.
Listen to their conversation. Where can Mike and Sue
do the following things?
For questions 1.-5. write a letter A-F in the correct box.

1. buy tickets ☐
2. see old rifles ☐
3. buy postcards ☐
4. have lunch ☐
5. find out about closing
   time ☐

A gift shop
B Winchester Firearms
  Museum
C information office
D ticket office
E Victorian Garden
F Winchester Café

2 Read this information about Sara Winchester. Then
complete the form.

Hello, my name is Sara Winchester. I'm 32 years old.
I was born in San Francisco, California. I am the manager of
the Winchester Rifle Company and I'm very rich.
I speak French, Spanish and German. I like talking to ghosts.

MANAGER OF THE YEAR

First Name:[1] *Sara* ....
Surname:[2] ....
Age:[3] ....
Place of birth:[4] ....
Nationality:[5] ....
Job:[6] ....
Foreign Language(s):[7] ....
Hobbies:[8] ....

3 Map Work

You have a map of part of California. The numbers represent the highways that take you to the Winchester Mystery House in San Jose and to other cities too. The American highway or freeway is the equivalent of the British motorway. American highways or freeways are free of charge.

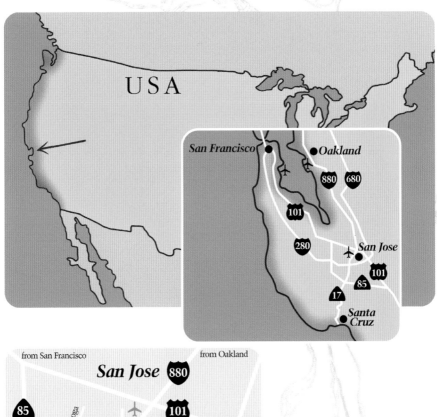

1. You are in San Francisco and you want to go to the Winchester Mystery House. You must go

☐ **A** north on 101 or 280.

☐ **B** south on 101 or 280.

☐ **C** south on 17.

2. Your friends live in Oakland. They want to meet you in San Jose. They must go

☐ **A** north on 680.

☐ **B** north on 880.

☐ **C** south on 880.

3. You're visiting a friend in Santa Cruz and you want to take him/her to the Winchester Mystery House. You must go

☐ **A** south on 101.

☐ **B** north on 17.

☐ **C** west on 17.

4. You live in San Jose and your friend invited you to a spooky Halloween party in Santa Cruz. You must go

☐ **A** south on 85.

☐ **B** east on 17.

☐ **C** south on 17.

5. A group of tourists is visiting the Winchester Mystery House. They want to go home and they live in San Francisco. They must go

☐ **A** north on 101 or 280.

☐ **B** south on 680.

☐ **C** north on 880.

Halloween Apple Cake

Makes about 12 slices

 175g flour

175g sugar

1 teaspoon of baking powder

 3 eggs

175g soft margarine

1 teaspoon of cinnamon [1]

50g chopped nuts

1 apple

Powdered sugar
for sprinkling [2] on top

1 20cm round,
loose-bottomed cake tin

1. Put the cake tin onto some greaseproof paper or baking paper. Draw around it and cut out the circle, just inside the line.

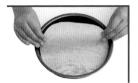

2. Put some margarine on the tin. Then put the paper into the bottom of it. Turn the oven on to 170° C.

3. Put the flour into a large bowl. Add the sugar and baking powder.

4. Break the eggs into a small bowl, then add them to the big bowl along with the margarine, cinnamon and half of the nuts.

---

1. **cinnamon** : 肉桂。

2. **sprinkling** : 撒。

5. Use a wooden spoon to mix everything together well. Put the mixture into the tin and smooth the top.

6. Peel the apple, then cut out the core. Cut the apple into thin slices. Lay the slices in circles on the top.

7. Sprinkle the apples with the remaining nuts and a tablespoon of powdered sugar. Bake the cake for an hour, until it is firm.

8. Leave the cake in the tin for ten minutes, before taking off the ring of the tin and lifting the cake off the base. Leave it to cool.

9. Use candied cherries to make a pumpkin face on the cake.

CHAPTER SEVEN

Spanish Spirits

María, Juan and Miguel Pereira lived in the village of Bélmez in southern Spain. They were farmers. On 23 August 1971 María Pereira was in the kitchen of her home. Suddenly she saw an image of a human face on the kitchen floor! She tried to wash the floor but the face did not go away. It became more visible. It was the sad face of a man with big eyes.

'Juan, come quickly! There is something strange on the kitchen floor!' María cried.

Her husband came quickly and looked at the floor. He was terrified.

'Oh, no! What is this? A human face! Call Miguel!' Juan said.

Their son Miguel looked at the floor and said, 'What's happening? This is macabre!'

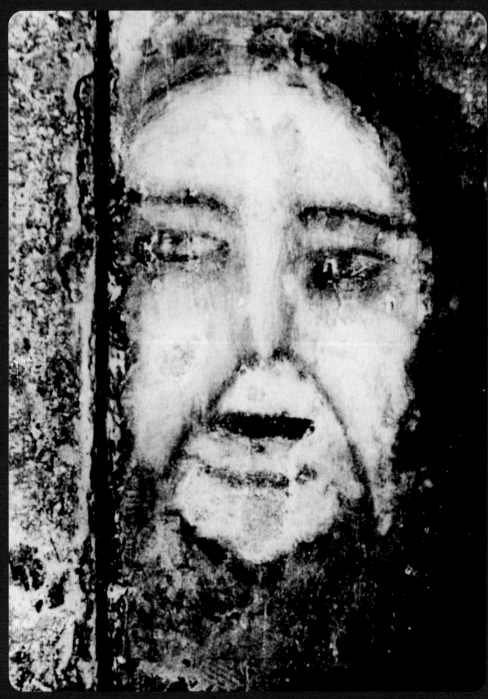

Bélmez de la Moraleda, Spain.
Dr. Elmar R. Gruber/Fortean Picture Library

Spanish Spirits

Miguel took a hammer [1] and destroyed part of the floor. But soon after another face appeared and then another. Miguel destroyed another part of the floor. But after a few days other faces appeared. There were faces of men, women and children of different ages. Sometimes small crosses [2] appeared too. At other times parts of the body were visible: a woman's hand with a flower.

Soon everyone in Bélmez knew about the mysterious faces. People came from other parts of Spain to see them. Many psychic experts were interested too. Professor de Argumosa of the University of Madrid started studying the faces. He also studied the chemical composition of the floor. But he found nothing unusual.

Professor de Argumosa discovered that in the 17th century the governor of Granada executed five people in Bélmez. But this was not a complete explanation because there were more than five faces.

Workmen started digging under the Pereira's house. They found many skeletons under the kitchen floor. Two skeletons were headless! Was this an old cemetery? Yes, it was. In the past there was a cemetery in the same place as the house. Perhaps the faces were the spirits of the dead in that cemetery.

Professor de Argumosa heard horrible cries and frightened voices in the Pereira kitchen. He made a recording of the cries and voices. He could also hear words in Spanish.

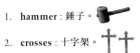

1. **hammer** : 錘子。
2. **crosses** : 十字架。

GHASTLY GHOSTS!

Experts from other countries went to Bélmez to study the mysterious faces. The psychic expert José Martinez Romero wrote a book about them. But no one has an answer...yet!

PHANTOM FILE

NUMBER 6

Where: ....

Name of the haunted place: ....

Number of ghosts: ....

Victims: Yes ☐ No ☐

If 'Yes', how many:................................

Your opinion: Haunted ☐ Not haunted ☐

Why: ....

....

....

UNDERSTANDING THE TEXT

1 **Read the paragraph and choose the best word (A, B, or C) for each space. The first is done for you.**

María Pereira was very ¹.......A....... when she saw an image of a human face ²................ the floor. She washed ³................, but the face ⁴................ not go away. No one could ⁵................ what was happening. There ⁶................ faces of men, women and children of ⁷................ ages. ⁸................ people and psychic experts came to Bélmez to see ⁹................ . Workmen began digging ¹⁰................ the Pereira house. They found ¹¹................ headless skeletons.

1. **A** surprised	**B** surprising	**C** surprise
2. **A** by	**B** over	**C** on
3. **A** them	**B** it	**C** him
4. **A** did	**B** does	**C** do
5. **A** understands	**B** understand	**C** understood
6. **A** were	**B** was	**C** is
7. **A** difference	**B** same	**C** different
8. **A** Many	**B** Much	**C** Few
9. **A** they	**B** them	**C** him
10. **A** under	**B** over	**C** near
11. **A** too	**B** two	**C** to

2 Professor de Argumosa wants to know more about the mysterious faces. Listen to this interview between María Pereira and Professor de Argumosa. For each question choose the correct answer A, B or C.

1. When did María see the face?

A ☐   B ☐   C ☐

2. What time was it?

A ☐   B ☐   C ☐

3. What was María doing?

A ☐   B ☐   C ☐

4. Who did María call?

A ☐   **B** ☐   **C** ☐

5. What was Miguel doing?

A ☐   **B** ☐   **C** ☐

3 Have fun with this crossword puzzle!

Across

3. You walk on it.

5. You cook here.

8. The dead are buried here.

9.

10. Not usual.

12. Bélmez is in .... .

13. Another word for ghost.

Down

1.

2. Opposite of present.

4.

6.

7. Mr and Mrs Pereira were .... .

11. Opposite of over.

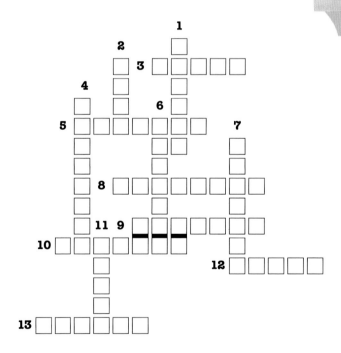

Literary Ghosts

Ghosts and the supernatural are part of literature. Let's meet some famous literary ghosts. William Shakespeare used ghosts in several of his plays. In *Hamlet,* the castle guards see the ghost of Hamlet's father one night. Then the ghost speaks to Hamlet and tells him terrible things about his murder.

Shakespeare's play *Macbeth* begins with three ugly witches. They tell Macbeth and Banquo strange things about their future. Later on in the play Banquo's ghost appears at a banquet table and scares Macbeth.

In *Richard III* the sad ghosts of two boy princes appear to King Richard. He murdered them earlier in the play.

In *Julius Caesar,* Caesar's ghost appears to remind Brutus of his crime.

The American writers Nathaniel Hawthorne and Edgar Allan Poe were very interested in the supernatural and in spirits. Their

Gertrude, Hamlet and the Ghost of Hamlet's Father *(1793)*
by Johann Heinrich Füssli.
Fondazione Magnani Rocca

Literary Ghosts

stories often talk about ghosts, evil spirits and demons. In Poe's stories death and the supernatural are often present. In *Eleonora* (1842), the ghost of Eleonora returns to give a message to the narrator.[1] In Hawthorne's novel *The House of the Seven Gables* (1851), unhappy people and strange spirits live in an evil, old house. His short story *Young Goodman Brown* (1846) talks about a young man and his adventure[2] in the forest with witches and the devil!

Charles Dickens' *A Christmas Carol* (1843) is a complete ghost story with four ghosts: Jacob Marley and the ghosts of Christmas Past, Christmas Present and Christmas Yet to Come. The ghost of Jacob Marley is an important character of the story.

Wilkie Collins was a writer and a friend of Charles Dickens. He was the father of the modern mystery story. He also wrote a complete ghost story called *The Haunted Hotel* (1879).

At the end of the 19th century the ghost story became a literary form. *The Canterville Ghost* (1887) by Oscar Wilde is an excellent example of a humorous ghost story. The ghost makes friends with one of the characters of the story.

In *The Turn of the Screw* (1898) Henry James created a macabre ghost story about two evil ghosts and their two young victims[3] – a very frightening tale!

---

1. **narrator**：講述者。
2. **adventure**：奇遇。
3. **victims**：受害者。

The Ghost of Christmas Yet to Come appears to Scrooge, from *A Christmas Carol.*

Ann Hodgkiss

UNDERSTANDING THE TEXT

1 Are these sentences **Right (A)** or **Wrong (B)**? If there is not enough information to answer **Right (A)** or **Wrong (B)**, choose **Doesn't Say (C)**. Circle the correct answer.

1. Wilkie Collins was the father of the modern mystery story.
   A Right   **B** Wrong   **C** Doesn't Say

2. Young Goodman Brown meets the witches and the devil in a cemetery.
   A Right   **B** Wrong   **C** Doesn't Say

3. *A Christmas Carol* is a story with three ghosts.
   A Right   **B** Wrong   **C** Doesn't Say

4. Oscar Wilde wrote a humorous ghost story.
   A Right   **B** Wrong   **C** Doesn't Say

5. The ghost of Eleonora is young and very beautiful.
   A Right   **B** Wrong   **C** Doesn't Say

6. Jacob Marley is a ghost.
   A Right   **B** Wrong   **C** Doesn't Say

7. Shakespeare's play *Richard III* begins with three ugly witches.
   A Right   **B** Wrong   **C** Doesn't Say

8. The American writers Hawthorne and Poe were interested in the supernatural.
   A Right   **B** Wrong   **C** Doesn't Say

9. Banquo's ghost appears in *Julius Caesar*.
   A Right   **B** Wrong   **C** Doesn't Say

10. The ghost of Julius Caesar has no head.
    A Right   **B** Wrong   **C** Doesn't Say

2 **Unscramble the words and put them in order to form a sentence.**

yulg   acbk   si   hednbi   erhet   na   opkos   ryuo

....

..............!

3 **When you think of a ghost, what colour(s) do you think of?**

....

....

....

....

4 **Now write your own description of a ghost.**

A ghost is ....

....

....

....

....

PHANTOM FILE

What are the results of the Phantom File?

a. Which was the scariest story? ....

....

Why? ....

....

....

b. Which of these ghosts would you like to meet? ....

....

Why? ....

....

....

c. Write a question or two to ask a ghost.

....

....

....

....

d. Do you know any ghost stories about where you live?
Write a short description of the story. Ask your teacher
or parents for help. Use 20-25 words.

....

....

....

....

....

EXIT TEST

1 **Read the information and write the name of the haunted place.**

a. Anne Boleyn was beheaded here. ....

b. Abraham Lincoln's ghost lives here. ....

c. There are images of human faces on the floor. ....

d. Lady Janet Glamis' ghost haunts its clock tower. ....

e. A horrible, evil ghost lives here. ....

f. This village has many ghosts. ....

g. The ghosts of two young princes haunt the stairs. ....

h. People see the ghost of a nun here. ....

2 **Are these sentences true (T) or false (F)? Correct the false ones.**

	T	F
a. Berkeley Square is in London.	☐	☐
b. Lord Lyttleton died at Berkeley Square.	☐	☐
c. The Earl of Glamis locked the men in a secret room.	☐	☐
d. A war destroyed Borley Rectory.	☐	☐
e. William the Conqueror built Glamis Castle.	☐	☐
f. The Winchester Mystery House is in California.	☐	☐
g. Nathaniel Hawthorne saw Reverend Harris' ghost at the White House.	☐	☐
h. John Wilkes Booth shot President Lincoln.	☐	☐
i. There was an old monastery under the Pereira's house.	☐	☐

3 **Complete the conversations. For each question choose the correct answer A, B or C.**

1. How old is the castle?
- **A** In 1500.
- **B** No, it's not.
- **C** Five hundred years old.

2. Is it haunted?
- **A** Yes, it's here.
- **B** It's very old.
- **C** Yes, it is.

3. How do you get to the castle?
- **A** It's far.
- **B** By bus.
- **C** In fifteen minutes.

4. Where is the nearest bus stop?
- **A** I don't know.
- **B** It's fine.
- **C** Thirty minutes.

5. How big is the secret room?
- **A** It's here.
- **B** It's very big.
- **C** Yes, it is.

6. What time does the castle open?
- **A** Three hours.
- **B** Since nine o'clock.
- **C** At ten o'clock.

4 **Where can you see these notices? For each question choose the correct answer A, B or C.**

1. Silence, please!
   - ☐ **A** In a restaurant.
   - ☐ **B** In a park.
   - ☐ **C** At the Atheneum library.

2. Danger! Don't use these stairs!
   - ☐ **A** At a zoo.
   - ☐ **B** At the Winchester House.
   - ☐ **C** At a beach.

3. Trains for Borley every 20 minutes.
   - ☐ **A** At a supermarket.
   - ☐ **B** At a station.
   - ☐ **C** At an airport.

4. Please don't talk to the ghosts!
   - ☐ **A** At a university.
   - ☐ **B** At a hotel.
   - ☐ **C** At the Tower of London.

5. Don't walk on this floor!
   - ☐ **A** At the Pereira House.
   - ☐ **B** At a cinema.
   - ☐ **C** On a plane.

6. Sleep here at your own risk.
   - ☐ **A** At a shoe shop.
   - ☐ **B** At 50 Berkeley Square.
   - ☐ **C** At a bakery.

COMPREHENSION TEST 1

 Circle the correct answer.

1. Who found a room full of skeletons?
   A. Lord Lyttleton　　**B.** Lady Glamis
   C. Lord Strathmore

2. Who didn't like the house at Berkeley Square?
   A. the older sailor　　**B.** Sara Winchester
   C. the younger sailor

3. Where is Borley Rectory?
   A. in Scotland　　**B.** 100 kilometres northeast of London
   C. in London

4. What was a favourite number with ghosts at the Winchester Mystery House?
   A. six　　**B.** thirteen　　**C.** one hundred

5. Who was King Henry VIII's second wife?
   A. Catherine Howard　　**B.** Jane Seymour
   C. Anne Boleyn

6. What was Abraham Lincoln's dream like?
   A. funny　　**B.** boring　　**C.** scary

7. Where did human faces appear on the kitchen floor?
   A. in Bélmez　　**B.** in Madrid　　**C.** in Granada

8. Which of the following is a ghost in a story?
   A. Henry James　　**B.** Jacob Marley　　**C.** Macbeth

9. Who was the Grey Lady?
   A. Anne Boleyn　　**B.** Marianne Foyster　　**C.** Lady Janet Glamis

COMPREHENSION TEST 2

6 **Read the paragraph and choose the best word (A, B or C) for each space; The first is done for you.**

In the United States ¹......B...... is the festivity of spirits and the supernatural. The Winchester Mystery House in San Jose, California is the ².............. monument to ghosts. Sara Winchester ³.............. a house in the ⁴.............. For thirty-six ⁵.............. she ⁶.............. a home for ghosts. Today it is has 160 rooms!

The ghosts of assassinated American ⁷..............haunt the White House. ⁸..............was the President of the United States ⁹.............. the American Civil War. He stopped ¹⁰..............in America but the southern states did not ¹¹.............. with him and he was assassinated while he was at the ¹².............. .

1.	**A** Thanksgiving	**B** Halloween	**C** Carnival
2.	**A** spookiest	**B** noisiest	**C** ugliest
3.	**A** brought	**B** buy	**C** bought
4.	**A** country	**B** city	**C** desert
5.	**A** days	**B** hours	**C** years
6.	**A** built	**B** build	**C** builds
7.	**A** cowboys	**B** presidents	**C** kings
8.	**A** Abraham Lincoln	**B** Nathaniel Hawthorne	**C** Reverend Harris
9.	**A** after	**B** before	**C** during
10.	**A** slavery	**B** witch hangings	**C** executions
11.	**A** vote	**B** agree	**C** complain
12.	**A** East Room	**B** White House	**C** theatre

KEY TO
THE EXERCISES
AND EXIT TEST

WHAT DO YOU KNOW ABOUT GHOSTS?

Page 9 – Exercise 1
a. F b. F c. F d. F e. F f. F
g. F h. T

CHAPTER 1
Understanding the text

Page 15 – Exercise 1
a. 4 b. 1 c. 5 d. 2

Page 15 – Exercise 2
a. ship   b. forest   c. spirit
d. old   e. machine   f. theatre

Page 15 – Exercise 3
a. machine   b. theatre   c. ship
d. old   e. forest

CHAPTER 2
Understanding the text

Page 22 – Exercise 1
1. A 2. B 3. C 4. B 5. A 6. A
7. C 8. B 9. A 10. B

Page 23 – Exercise 2
1. C 2. B 3. A 4. C 5. C 6. C
7. B 8. C

Page 24 – Exercise 3
1. C 2. B 3. A 4. C 5. B

CHAPTER 3
Understanding the text

Page 30 – Exercise 1
1. E 2. A 3. C 4. G 5. D
6. F 7. B

Page 32 – Exercise 2
a. unexplored / b. unkind /
c. unnecessary / d. unable /
e. unhealthy / f. unknown / g. unlocked

CHAPTER 4
Understanding the text

Page 41 – Exercise 1
2. A 3. C 4. B 5. C 6. B
7. C 8. A 9. C 10. A 11. B

Page 42 – Exercise 2
1. E 2. G 3. A 4. F 5. C 6. D

Page 43 – Exercise 3

A	D	G	E	P	V	L	K	J	F	Y	R	C
H	O	L	L	I	N	G	S	W	O	R	T	H
C	S	B	Z	N	D	H	O	Q	Y	H	J	A
X	L	D	E	G	L	C	W	K	S	T	G	I
O	Y	F	L	P	C	Z	E	N	T	I	S	Z
H	E	M	J	Q	O	S	S	I	E	N	M	X
Z	O	G	A	E	F	T	G	Z	R	A	I	H
K	I	N	C	R	O	G	T	C	I	S	T	O
R	V	I	O	U	D	R	U	E	V	Q	H	A
M	R	Z	T	B	U	L	L	U	R	V	O	R
P	X	M	F	S	R	U	B	A	L	O	B	W

83

Page 43 – Exercise 4
a. Foyster   **b.** Hollingsworth and Potter   **c.** Bull   **d.** Price   **e.** Smith

CHAPTER 5
Understanding the text

Page 49 – Exercise 1
1. Tower   **2.** father   **3.** guide
4. axe   **5.** head   **6.** sword
7. execution   **8.** visitors/tourists

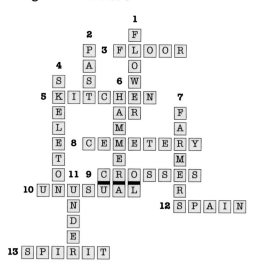

Page 49 – Exercise 2
1. small and cold   **2.** one
3. a table, a chair and a bed
4. one meal a day   **5.** some bread and some milk   **6.** three

Page 50 – Exercise 3
a. any / **b.** some / **c.** any / **d.** Some / **e.** any / **f.** any / **g.** some

CHAPTER 6
Understanding the text

Page 58 – Exercise 1
1. D   **2.** B   **3.** A   **4.** F   **5.** C

Page 58 – Exercise 2
2. Winchester   **3.** 32 years old
4. San Francisco, California
5. American   **6.** manager of the Winchester Rifle Company
7. French, Spanish and German
8. talking to ghosts

Page 59 – Exercise 3
1. B   **2.** C   **3.** B   **4.** C   **5.** A

CHAPTER 7
Understanding the text

Page 67 – Exercise 1
2. C   **3.** B   **4.** A   **5.** B   **6.** A
7. C   **8.** A   **9.** B   **10.** A   **11.** B

Page 68 – Exercise 2
1. B   **2.** C   **3.** A   **4.** C   **5.** A

Page 70 – Exercise 3

CHAPTER 8
Understanding the text

Page 75 – Exercise 1
1. A   **2.** B   **3.** B   **4.** A   **5.** C   **6.** A
7. B   **8.** A   **9.** B   **10.** C

Page 76 – Exercise 2
There is an ugly spook behind your back!

Page 78 – Exercise 1

a. Tower of London / **b.** The White House / **c.** Bélmez, Spain / **d.** Glamis Castle / **e.** Berkeley Square / **f.** Borley / **g.** Tower of London / **h.** Borley

Page 78 – Exercise 2

a. T   b. F   c. T   d. F   e. F   f. T
g. F   h. T   i. F

Page 79 – Exercise 3

1. C   2. C   3. B   4. A   5. B   6. C

Page 80 – Exercise 4

1. C   2. B   3. B   4. C   5. A   6. B

Page 81 – Comprehension Test 1

1. C   2. A   3. B   4. B   5. C
6. C   7. A   8. B   9. C

Page 82 – Comprehension Test 2

2. A   3. C   4. A   5. C   6. A
7. B   8. A   9. C   10. A   11. B
12. C

Black Cat English Readers

BLACK CAT ENGLISH CLUB
Membership Application Form

BLACK CAT ENGLISH CLUB is for those who love English reading and seek for better English to share and learn with fun together.

Benefits offered: - *Membership Card*

- *Member badge, poster, bookmark*
- *Book discount coupon*
- *Black Cat English Reward Scheme*
- *English learning e-forum*
- *Surprise gift and more...*

Simply fill out the application form below and fax it back to 2565 1113.

Join Now! It's FREE exclusively for readers who have purchased *Black Cat English Readers* !

The book(or book set) that you have purchased: _____

English Name: _____ (Surname) _____ (Given Name)

Chinese Name: _____

Address: _____

Tel: _____ Fax: _____

Email: _____

Sex: ❏ Male   ❏ Female   (Login password for e-forum will be sent to this email address.)

Education Background: ❏ Primary 1-3   ❏ Primary 4-6   ❏ Junior Secondary Education (F1-3)

❏ Senior Secondary Education (F4-5)   ❏ Matriculation

❏ College   ❏ University or above

Age: ❏ 6 - 9   ❏ 10 - 12   ❏ 13 - 15   ❏ 16 - 18   ❏ 19 - 24   ❏ 25 - 34

❏ 35 - 44   ❏ 45 - 54   ❏ 55 or above

Occupation: ❏ Student   ❏ Teacher   ❏ White Collar   ❏ Blue Collar

❏ Professional   ❏ Manager   ❏ Business Owner   ❏ Housewife

❏ Others (please specify: _____)

As a member, what would you like **BLACK CAT ENGLISH CLUB** to offer:

❏ Member gathering/ party   ❏ English class with native teacher   ❏ English competition

❏ Newsletter   ❏ Online sharing   ❏ Book fair

❏ Book discount   ❏ Others (please specify: _____)

Other suggestions to **BLACK CAT ENGLISH CLUB**:

_____

Please sign here: _____

(Date: _____)